The Twelfth Night Santons

The
Twelfth Night
Santons

By
MARION GARTHWAITE

Illustrated by
WINIFRED LUBELL

Doubleday & Company, Inc., Garden City, New York

Library of Congress Catalog Card Number 64-18227
Text Copyright © 1965 by Marion Garthwaite
Illustrations Copyright © 1965 by Winifred Lubell
All Rights Reserved
Printed in the United States of America
First Edition

To
Margaret Lesser,
friend, editor, mentor

About Santons

In the Christmas season many families set up a little manger scene, or crèche, with the Holy Family, the animals of the stable, and the three kings who brought their gifts to the Christ Child on the twelfth night after Christmas.

In Provence, where people call the little statues in the crèches *santons,* many other figures have been added over the years—a mayor, a drummer, dozens of workers, all bringing a gift for the Child. Most of the santons have traditional names, and new characters are added only after careful consideration.

Many families in Provence work all year making santons to sell at Christmas, as they have done for more than a century. Santons are made of soft clay which is pressed into molds, hardened or baked, and then painted. They come in many sizes from a foot high down to figures so small they are called *quart de puce* (a quarter of a flea).

The village children of St. Croix called Pierre that fool of a cloud gazer.

"In very truth he forgets to herd the sheep," they said. "It is the sheep who look out for Pierre. When it is time to come home, the sheep turn from their browsing. They bleat. The bells jangle down the path. Only then Pierre remembers to follow them home. A born fool, Pierre."

Pierre was small for his age, with a knee that stiffened in the cold. That and his brooding eyes set him apart from the other shepherd boys. But Pierre was a whirlwind when he was teased. He bit and gouged and kicked, until the other boys were glad to let him alone. Those who had taken a chew of that sour apple did not want another bite.

"Leave him alone," they warned. "His lameness makes him mean."

It was not the lameness with Pierre. It was something else. Something inside of him. Pierre did not like to herd sheep. He hated the stupid beasts. Only the newborn lambs he liked—so gay, so full of grace, so beautiful in their young spring leaping. He liked the clouds because they made pictures in the sky. He liked the field flowers because the colors shouted at him.

Pierre had long wished to make the santons, the small figures that many of the villagers molded or carved to sell at Christmas time. But when he asked his uncle, Jacques growled at him, "It is for you to guard the sheep."

When Pierre had driven the sheep up the steep path to where the grass was uncropped, he had nothing else to do. He forgot the sheep. He sat on the hillside staring at the clouds, watching them make and unmake a dozen pictures in an hour's time. As he watched, his fingers gathered up the moist earth beside him, pressing it into little santon shapes that pleased him. Shapes, alas, that fell apart into gritty mud in his fingers. Mud is not clay to mold and stretch and engrave with tools.

Pierre yearned for a knife with which to whittle and carve. But where would an orphan shepherd boy find enough pennies for a knife?

This year the Mayor of St. Croix had offered
a prize for the best santons made of the three
kings who had brought their gifts to the Christ
Child on Twelfth Night. The prize would be
given at the Feast of the Epiphany, when the
three kings would have finished their journey
and could be added to the many little figures
gathered about the mangers set up on the tables
in every home.

Now the days were short. The keen wind of
the first winter days cut through Pierre's sheep-
skin coat. With the first snow the ewes would be
penned. Only the breeding stock would be winter-
fed. Each day Pierre searched the leaden skies
for the first signs of snow that would free him
of the herding.

"It is too cold for snow!" growled Pierre's
uncle Jacques.

The Advent lights, twisted wicks of grass in cups of oil, were already set in the windows to light the way for the Holy Child. In most households in Provence the villagers were setting up their own santons, the small figures for the manger scenes that graced even the meanest hut at Christmastide. Whole families made the santons during the long winter evenings, for their own crèches or to sell to tourists who stopped off at the market.

Jacques, the uncle with whom Pierre lived, did not make santons. Instead, in the long winter evenings he cut and stitched sheepskins into bags and jackets.

"It is for you to soften the skins," he told Pierre, gruffly.

Pierre hated the smell of tallow and the feel of the rough hides. He thought he could never get away from sheep.

If only it would snow, he thought in the morning, as he opened the stable door at the other end of his uncle's house. He drove the sheep up the road on their way to the meadows higher up the mountain.

When he reached the last house at the end of the village Pierre came upon Papa Gant, who was old and bent and nearly blind. Three hulking shepherd boys were teasing the old man. They had pinned a paper to his back which read, "I am a fool. Kick me, if you please!"

With great snortings and chokings of laughter the boys pranced about Papa Gant, just out of reach of his flailing cane.

Pierre sailed in. With a well-aimed kick he sent one boy sprawling in the ditch. He punched another in the nose and the boy backed off. The last one caught Pierre by his hair, twisting his head back. Papa Gant struck the bigger boy with his cane, sending him bawling after his sheep.

As Pierre unpinned the paper, Papa Gant peered closely at him. "It is Pierre, the nephew of Jacques?"

"Yes, sir."

"Your uncle tells me you would like to make santons, Pierre, eh?"

"Oh yes, oh yes, sir!"

The old man sighed. "If I had money for clay, of a certainty I would teach you to make santons. Come to my house this evening when the sheep are safely home. I will show you my crèche and my santons."

Pierre's heart was singing as he drove the sheep up the rocky path. He had routed his enemies. He had helped Papa Gant. Tonight he was going to the house of Papa Gant, who made the finest santons in all St. Croix.

All day Pierre thought of santons. The Holy Infant, gentle Mary, the shepherds. And the three kings who were moved up little by little, each of the twelve days after Christmas. There was the young king, Gaspar of Tarsus, with the myrrh in a golden horn. Balthasar, dark-skinned king of Ethiopia, who brought the frankincense.

And old Melchior, King of Arabia, offering his casket of gold.

In the clouds Pierre pictured them. One standing straight and tall, one bowing toward the manger, and the last one kneeling, having come at last before the little Jesus at the Feast of the Epiphany.

When Pierre reached home that night his
uncle drove him from the house with angry
words. "Fourteen sheep go with you, and you
bring back twelve." His voice rose. "No one has
wits enough to make santons who cannot even
count sheep." He shoved Pierre out of the stable
door. "No supper, no bed—you dolt—until you
find my sheep."

Pierre limped back up the steep trail. Sheep!
How he hated them. Still, he remembered, there
were always sheep among the santons. One ox,
one ass, three sheep. Perhaps the Baby Jesus
liked sheep. Pierre, worried, wondered if it might
be a sin for him to hate the stupid beasts the
way he did.

He found the two ewes in a gully by the stream where he had watered them. One of them was bogged down in the heavy soil. Pierre had to dig her hoofs out with his bare hands. The night wind was bitter. The ewe kicked and struggled, bleating.

When she was free, the sheep trotted off along the trail. Pierre stumbled down from the meadow and locked the beasts in the stable.

A few minutes later he was knocking at the door of the thatched hut of Papa Gant.

"Enter, then!"

Pierre pushed off his muddy wood-soled shoes before the door. The house inside was warm with many candles burning, more candles than Pierre had ever seen lighted at one time. It made the room seem bright and gay. Then he remembered that Papa Gant was nearly blind and needed more light.

The old man put before Pierre a steaming bowl of onion soup. There were browned bread crusts on top of it, and grated goat's cheese.

Pierre thought he should be polite. He said he had eaten.

Papa Gant refused to listen. "A growing boy needs food at all hours. Eat then, since the santons will wait for you."

When Pierre could not push into his mouth another bite, Papa Gant led him to the end of the room. Here the crèche had been set up on a smaller table.

Pierre, entranced, stared at each santon in turn. None of them was more than two inches high. The Infant Jesus lay on the straw of a tiny manger, with Mary and Joseph kneeling beside him. From an open window in the house above the manger a small figure gazed down at the scene in the manger below, his arms upraised in

astounded joy. On the roof were a cock and hens. Below again there were the ox, the ass, three sheep. There were angels and shepherds. There were a well, a bridge, a sanctuary. A hill of packed earth covered with tiny trees had been shaped to hide the three kings until Twelfth Night.

"Oh, sir! It is a crèche of great magnificence!"

Coming toward the manger on all sides were
the villagers—the knife grinder, the fish vendor,
the miller with his sack of flour on his shoulder.
A blind man was guided by his small son. Mar-
garido sat upon a gray donkey, spinning as she
rode. An old wood-gatherer, bent beneath her

bundle of tiny sticks, was bringing these as her
gift. Never had Pierre seen so many figures so
carefully wrought. Each santon was painted with
bright and living colors.

"*C'est du bon, non?*" asked Papa Gant.

"Oh, yes. It is beautiful!"

"But see!" The old man looked sorry as he picked up three empty molds. "I cannot finish my three kings. The molds are made, but foolishly I sold the first models." He lifted his shoulders and spread his hands. "A crèche I have, but no kings to move up each day. No clay."

"Surely, sir, you could spare a few pennies for clay."

"*Non!*" Papa Gant shook his head stubbornly. His lined and flabby cheeks trembled. His thin lips were set. "*Non!* Every penny, each single penny must go to the eye doctor. When I save enough he will take off this blindness. And then I shall see to make a thousand santons."

"But if your three kings took the mayor's prize, sir? That money would pay the doctor."

Papa Gant shook his head. "I must wait, for God is in the waiting."

Pierre took the empty molds in his hands. He felt a deep sadness to think that with this beautiful crèche there were no kings to bring the gifts to the Christ Child.

The next day the heavy clouds broke up. They turned and curdled in the sky. The air was warmer. By late afternoon the first snowflakes were falling—crisp, tiny crystals like stars. On the wool of Pierre's smock they stayed long enough to delight him with their fragile beauty.

With his face tiptilted to catch the cold flakes on his lips, and his thoughts on santons, he followed the sheep across the stream and down the meadow path to St. Croix.

45

There he met his uncle with a willow switch in his hand. "Imbecile! Of a stupidity, head of a cabbage! Again the sheep come home untended, and one missing!"

He struck Pierre across the legs with the switch. Pierre felt the blows little enough beneath the strips of woolen cloth that bound his legs. But he felt keenly the guffaws of laughter from the other shepherd boys coming down from the meadows.

"Pierre watches the skies instead of the sheep!" they taunted. "That cloud gazer!"

"Go back and find the ewe," ordered his uncle. "Do not come home without her."

Pierre turned wearily back up the steep path. His knee ached. His mind smarted from the blows and the laughter. The snow blew in his face, wet and cold. Sheep!

He found the ewe where she had been lost before. This time she was down, feebly bleating, her forelegs stuck in the heavy soil. Pierre picked up a stick. He was angry at his uncle for beating him. He was angry at the boys for laughing at him. He was angry at himself for carelessness. He raised the stick to strike the hindquarters of the helpless ewe.

Her eyes beseeched Pierre for help. She struggled up and sank again, her head stretched out on the cold ground. She shut her eyes against the stick.

Something stayed Pierre's hand. It is as though she prays, he thought. He remembered the sheep kneeling before the crèche of the good Papa Gant. He threw away the stick. Carefully, gently, he raised the ewe. It took a long time. The snow fell steadily. His hands were icy cold.

When she was safely out of the mud, he led her through the stream. He washed the clinging soil from her legs. He washed his own hands in the freezing water. The earth stuck to his fingers, slick and greasy.

It is like clay, he thought. Clay! It *is* clay! This is a clay bed where the ewe has been. "It's *clay!*" he shouted to the falling snow. The word sang in his ears. Clay for old Papa Gant who must save every penny to save his eyes.

Pierre gathered a great handful of the heavy earth, rolling it into a stiff, elastic ball. When the ewe was penned with the others, he ran to the house of Papa Gant.

"Papa Gant! Papa Gant!" he shouted.

"*Sacré bleu!* Must you shout to heaven?"

Pierre placed the lump of clay in Papa Gant's gnarled hands. "Clay, Papa Gant! Truly it is clay. The ewe was lost there. Feel of it. Clay for your three kings."

Papa Gant felt it. He pushed and kneaded it in his fingers. "You speak truth. It is good clay. Where did you find this clay?"

Pierre told him how, twice now, the ewe had bogged down in the stream bed. "Twice, sir, she led me to this clay."

The old man was pleased. "Bring me more of this fine clay, Pierre. Tomorrow we shall make santons."

The next night Papa Gant showed Pierre what must be done with clay. He had allowed it to harden. Now it was crushed with a heavy mallet and screened. Water was added, little by little, to make a stiff dough.

"Now, Pierre, it must be cut." Over and over the clay was thrown against a tight wire to be sliced in two. It was turned and slapped together and cut again and again.

"Why must we do all this, Papa Gant?"

"We want no air bubbles to crack and spoil our santons. The clay must be smooth inside and out."

There was a banging at the door. "Who is it, then?" shouted Papa Gant.

"It is I, Jacques." Pierre's uncle pushed open the door. The candles guttered as the snow swirled into the room. "What are you doing here, Pierre?"

"He is working," answered Papa Gant. "You have said he is no good with sheep. Let us see how he is with clay."

Clutching the lump of clay to his chest, Pierre watched his uncle blink in the candlelight. He felt like the ewe bogged down in the stream bed, waiting for the stick to strike.

· "While the snow lasts, then—" his uncle grumbled.

As the door closed behind Jacques, Pierre let out a long sigh and threw the lump of clay against the wire.

When the clay felt right, Papa Gant pushed a small lump of it into one of the molds for the three kings. He tied the two halves together with strips of cloth.

"We shall not bake these three kings," he told Pierre. "There is no time now to take them to the kiln. When they are hard, we shall smooth and trim them and paint them as they are. Later you will learn how to bake clay and make glazes."

Papa Gant finished binding together his three molds.

"Now then, Pierre!" Papa Gant set his three molds on the deep window sill. "What will you choose to make? Into what will you mold this clay for your first santon? Will it be an angel, perhaps? A villager? The Blessed Virgin?"

Pierre shook his head. "No, sir. None of these." His eyes were shining in the candlelight.

"I shall make a sheep. A sheep with fleece as white as summer clouds. For my first santon I shall make a sheep—" his voice dropped to a whisper—"a kneeling sheep."

His fingers worked with a lump of clay. This was not crumbly mud to fall apart in his hands. He molded a small oval for a stand to hold his santon. He would paint this the soft green of the meadow grass.

He rolled and pressed the clay, closing his eyes to see in his mind the ewe kneeling in the stream. His fingers were sure as he pinched off clay for ears and tail. He took one of the pointed sticks from the table to rough up the skin to look like wool, and to shape the eyes and mouth.

At last he leaned back.

"It is done, then?" asked Papa Gant.

"It is finished."

Papa Gant pushed a candle close to Pierre's santon, peering at it. "It is a good santon, Pierre."

Pierre nodded, blinking sleepily. "It is the sheep who found the clay for your three kings. It is her gift for the Child on Twelfth Night."

Marion Garthwaite is a Californian, but she felt very much at home writing about the santons of Provence. She has visited there, and for many years her set of some twenty santons has been "a part of Christmas." Her santons are also a part of this book, since she lent them to the artist for models.

Mrs. Garthwaite served for many years as children's librarian, both in Madera, where she and her husband raised their two children, and in Menlo Park, where she now lives. She has also turned her favorite hobby — storytelling — to such professional uses as radio programs, the classroom and, of course, writing books for young people.

Winifred Lubell was born in New York City, and now lives in Croton-on-Hudson, New York. She and her husband have two sons, and "lots of pets." She has illustrated many books, including several written by her husband.

Mrs. Lubell has also visited Provence, and her affection for that region is reflected in her charming pictures for this book.